ELK GROVE VILLAGE

3 1250 0071 3675

S0-ARJ-719

Editor: Christianne Jones
Page Production: Tracy Davies
Creative Director: Keith Griffin
Editorial Director: Carol Jones
Managing Editor: Catherine Neitge

First American edition published in 2006 by
Picture Window Books
5115 Excelsior Boulevard
Suite 232
Minneapolis, MN 55416
877-845-8392
www.picturewindowbooks.com

Copyright © 2004 by Allegra Publishing Limited
Unit 13/15 Quayside Lodge
William Morris Way
Townmead Road
London SW6 2UZ
UK

The art in this book was colored by Datagraph System.

Printed in the United States of America.

Library of Congress Cataloging-in-Publication Data
Law, Felicia.
Rumble meets Penny Panther / by Felicia Law ; illustrated by Yoon-Mi Pak.—1st
American ed.
p. cm. — (Read-it! readers)
Summary: The beautiful and elegant Penny Panther, hired by Rumble the Dragon to
run the gift shop in his Cave Hotel, convinces her new boss to do her work for her.
ISBN 1-4048-1331-4 (hard cover)
[1. Friendship—Fiction. 2. Panthers—Fiction. 3. Dragons—Fiction.] I. Pak,
Yoon-Mi, ill. II. Title. III. Series.

PZ7.L41835Rump 2005
[E]—dc22
2005007362

Rumble Meets Penny Panther

by Felicia Law
illustrated by Yoon-Mi Pak

Special thanks to our advisers for their expertise:

Adria F. Klein, Ph.D.
Professor Emeritus, California State University
San Bernardino, California

Susan Kesselring, M.A.
Literacy Educator
Rosemount–Apple Valley–Eagan (Minnesota) School District

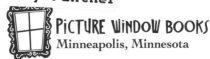

PiCTURE WiNDOW BOOKS
Minneapolis, Minnesota

This is a story of a cool, young dragon named Rumble. When his grandma leaves her run-down cave to him, Rumble sets about making it into a four-star hotel. He doesn't do it all alone. He has help from a picky hotel inspector and an annoying spider named Shelby.

Rumble's Cave Hotel is about to open its very own shop called String of Pearls. The shop will offer guests the very best in fashion and will be run by the elegant Penny Panther. But will this pretty cat do any work?

Penny Panther leaned on the manager's desk and filed her long, red claws.

"Excuse me," said Rumble. "I'm the manager of Rumble's Cave Hotel. Can I help you?"

"You can," purred Penny. "You're such a fine gentleman. I'm sure you can help a beautiful lady in distress."

"Distress?" asked Rumble.

"I'm hot and dusty after my journey," said Penny. "I need to freshen up."

"I need a bubble bath, a fluffy towel, a facial, skin cleanser, shampoo, nail clippers, and a massage table. And most of all, I need a bottle of sparkling water!" said Penny.

"OK. And who are you?" Rumble asked.

"I'm Miss Penny Panther, the beautiful Miss Panther, at your service," said Penny in a silky voice, as she fluttered her eyelashes at Rumble.

"But of course," said Rumble. "What a perfectly gorgeous, charming, attractive, graceful, elegant, stylish charmer you are."

"She was hired to run the gift shop," hissed Shelby Spider.

"Of course," said Rumble.

"I sure hope you can count or the shop will make no money," Shelby said.

"Don't worry," purred Penny. "There are lots of clever things a girl can do, just you wait and see."

"Hmm!" said Shelby. "Hmm!"

13

Penny stood in the cluttered shop. There were boxes piled from the floor to the ceiling. The goods were all there—boxes, and boxes, and boxes of them.

"I wonder if you would help me unpack the boxes," said Penny, fluttering her eyelashes. "They're SO heavy. I don't want to break a nail."

Rumble said he was happy to help. "Leave it to me," he said. "I'll unpack it all."

"Too kind," purred Penny.

"Too silly," sighed Shelby.

Penny stood among the piles of goods. The shelves were all empty—rows, and rows, and rows of shelves.

"I wonder if you would help me fill the shelves," said Penny, fluttering her eyelashes. "They're SO high. I don't want to hurt my back."

Rumble said he was happy to help. "Leave it to me," he said. "I'll fill the shelves."

"Too kind," purred Penny.

"Too silly," sighed Shelby.

Penny stood in front of the cash register.
Coins were piled high—lots, and lots, and
lots of coins.

"I wonder if you would help me count the
coins," said Penny, fluttering her eyelashes.
"They're SO dirty. I don't want to dirty
my hands."

Rumble said he was happy to help. "Leave it
to me," he said. "I'll count the coins."

"Too kind," purred Penny.

"Too silly," sighed Shelby.

Rumble stood in the shop. He had unpacked the stock, filled the shelves, and counted the coins. Penny sat behind the counter, filing her long, red claws.

"Hello!" called Shelby. "Can anyone help me?"

Penny didn't move. "Sorry, I'm busy," she said.

"I want to buy socks," said Shelby.
"Small ones."

"I have hats," said Penny. "Let me show you
hats. I also have shawls, shirts, and gowns."

"Socks!" said Shelby. "I just want socks!"

"Tights?" asked Penny. "In red?"

"That shop is no good," Shelby told Rumble. "It's been open all day, and you haven't sold a thing. Look! The cash register is completely empty."

"Funny," said Rumble. "It had lots of coins in it this morning. Maybe Penny took them."

"I'm sure she did," said Shelby.

Penny sat in the restaurant in her flashing jewelry and her beautiful zebra-skin coat.

A large bottle of sparkling water stood on the table. Two glasses stood nearby.

"You see!" Rumble told Shelby. "Penny is waiting for me. She took the coins to buy me some fancy water. What a kind thought."

"Sorry," said Penny, "the sparkling water is for my gentleman friend."

"Your friend?" asked Shelby.

"Yes, my friend," said Penny.

"I told you not to trust her," said Shelby.

"I thought she liked me," sighed Rumble.

"You should stick to your old friends," said Shelby. "The ones you can trust."

"I don't have any friends," sighed Rumble.

"But I'm your friend," said Shelby. "Who cooked dead flies for you when you were hungry? Me. Of course I'm your friend. I'm your BEST friend."

Rumble looked at Penny Panther. Then he looked at his old friend Shelby Spider. Penny was beautiful, but she wasn't a good friend. Shelby was annoying, but she was a great friend.

"I guess you're right," Rumble said to Shelby. "Old friends are the best friends."

More *Read-it!* Readers

Bright pictures and fun stories help you practice your reading skills. Look for more books at your level.

Happy Birthday, Gus! by Jacklyn Williams
Happy Easter, Gus! by Jacklyn Williams
Happy Halloween, Gus! by Jacklyn Williams
Happy Thanksgiving, Gus! by Jacklyn Williams
Happy Valentine's Day, Gus! by Jacklyn Williams
Matt Goes to Mars by Carole Tremblay
Merry Christmas, Gus! by Jacklyn Williams
Rumble Meets Buddy Beaver by Felicia Law
Rumble Meets Eli Elephant by Felicia Law
Rumble Meets Keesha Kangaroo by Felicia Law
Rumble Meets Penny Panther by Felicia Law
Rumble Meets Wally Warthog by Felicia Law

Looking for a specific title or level? A complete list of *Read-it!* Readers is available on our Web site:
www.picturewindowbooks.com